THE ARRANGEMENT
VOL. 2

H.M. Ward

www.SexyAwesomeBooks.com
Laree Bailey Press

Laree Bailey Press
ISBN 1482628961
First Edition: Feb 2013

THE ARRANGEMENT

VOL. 2

CHAPTER 1

Sean's eyes are locked with mine. He doesn't react to my words. There's no smile on his lips, no sense of relief or joy. Instead, he stays a breath from my lips with his fingers gently brushing my cheek. His other hand is possessively holding me against his waist. His body is so hard. My thoughts keep drifting to running my tongue over his firm stomach. It makes my toes curl and I feel shy, but I don't look away from him.

No one has ever looked at me like this. I mean, it's not a gaze that's tender and sweet. Sean's eyes are filled with desire that darkens by the second. It's like his eyes could devour me whole. That carnal look makes my body grow warmer. My heart slams into my ribs like it's trying to save itself, like it knows Sean's bad for me.

I don't know what I expect Sean to do, but he's slow about doing it. He teases me, leaving his lips so close to mine that I tremble. By the time Sean closes the distance between us, I can barely control myself. He brushes his bottom lip against mine. The electricity that's been building between us ignites and I suck in startled breath. My legs feel like they want to run, but I can't. My muscles twitch like my fight or flight response is taking over, but I force the sensation back. There is no way Sean will hurt me. Miss Black made it clear that she'll hurt him if something happens to me. My heart on the other hand, well that's a different issue.

I stand there as Sean's body is pressed tighter to mine. Every curve, every muscle, slips into place until there is no space between us. His body is rock hard and so warm. I feel him under the supple fabric and know how much he wants me.

Sean's fingers gently tangle in my curls, as he brushes his lips past mine again. The floor of my stomach falls away and it feels like I'm falling. The kiss is so light, so perfect. It makes me lightheaded like I'm drunk and as soon as his mouth is gone, I want more. My eyes flutter open. I didn't realize that I'd closed them.

Sean pulls back and watches me with that intense gaze. It burns a trail between my eyes and my lips. Sean tilts his head in and rests his forehead against mine, locking our eyes. I feel his rib cage expand as he sucks in a jagged breath. Excitement is brimming beneath the surface, barely contained.

I don't know what I want or what I want him to do. My mind is lost in a cavern of lust and I can't find my way out. Hell, I don't even know if I want out. My life sucks and this little reprieve is heaven. There's no reason to think, nothing to worry about. After this tryst, I'll have what I need as well as plenty of memories to keep me warm on cold nights. So why am I trembling? What am I afraid of? I made peace with this decision. *Yeah, keep telling yourself that*, a bitter voice says at the back of my mind.

It takes me a moment, but I realize that Sean frightens me in a way that I can't fathom. Most of the fears in my life are tangible, but this one isn't. My emotions feel dazed, like they don't know what's real and what's fake. Sean doesn't really love me. I don't love him, but still—there's something there and it calls to me.

The way his eyes drink me in, the way his hands feel on my skin, and the way he teases makes me crazy—I've never reacted to a guy like this in my entire life. There was never any heat, not even a spark. That's what makes things with Sean all the more insane. From day one, I felt something for him. He walked into my life and filled a hole that I didn't even know was there. It's too soon for that. A couple of kisses and smiles later, and I sound like I'm ready to marry the guy. What the hell is wrong with me?

Sean watches me closely as I think. Every time I take a breath in, my breasts press harder against his chest. It feels right. I want more. As if he can read my mind, Sean lowers his lashes with his gaze fixated on my lips. When he lowers his mouth to meet mine, the thoughts rush from my mind. Like a surging river they race through, and are gone before I can blink.

Sean's fingers drift down to my cheek and he tilts my head to the side. My heart pounds harder in my chest. His lips are full and soft. They seek mine, applying the perfect amount of pressure and the kiss deepens. I push my body against his chest and my arms wrap around his neck. I play with the hair at the base of his neck as he kisses me, feeling the silky strands slip between my fingers.

As we kiss, a thought races through my mind, a warning. Something about kissing. It flutters through my mind, unclear. Sean licks the seam of my lips once, and then twice. My heart races harder as he does it. I'm ready to open my mouth and let him kiss me deeper. I want it. I want him. My body is charged, ready for that kiss. Every inch of me is tingling. There's a wave of desire building inside of me and his kiss will set it free.

His kiss. Kissing…

"I can't," I say into his mouth as the memory hits me. Gasping, I pull away and turn my face.

CHAPTER 2

The kiss breaks. I can barely breathe. The rapid pace of my heart won't slow. My hands tremble at his neck and there's no way to hide it. I pull away from him and cold air fills the space, chilling me. "I'm sorry."

Sean says nothing at first. He watches me. I feel his eyes slip over my body. They take in the slight tremor, the way I wrap my arms around my middle, and the way I can't look him in the eye. Instead of demanding my services, Sean slips back into his chair like he doesn't mind. "There's nothing to apologize for."

I glance at him from over my shoulder. I don't believe him. My gaze says as much.

Sean smiles at me. "It's part of the package, Miss Smith. Skittish virgins are appealing." It's the look he gave me when my car broke down. Something about the way he gazes at me makes me feel like I'm in emotional overload.

My face flushes and I glance away. What was I thinking? I can't do this. I can't be with him, not when he affects me like this. The whole sex thing is a pastime to him, but to me it isn't. I took this job because I needed the money, but even more so, I took this job because I have feelings for Sean. I like the way he makes me feel. I want to know him better. I want him to be mine.

That's not what this is.

The trembling becomes more noticeable. Sean stands and walks up behind me, rubbing his hands over my arms. He presses a kiss to my temple and holds me. "Your preferences said kissing on the lips was off limits. I shouldn't have done it. I apologize."

"You went straight for the only thing you couldn't have?" I did mark that on the sheet. Kissing forms attachments. I can't be attached to him. *You already are*, a voice says inside my head. *Go to hell*, I answer, already knowing it's true. I feel his gaze on the side of my face.

Holding me tightly, Sean says, "It's my nature. I'm sorry, Avery. It won't happen again, not unless you ask me to kiss you."

As he speaks, his warm breath breezes past my ear. I shiver in his arms and feel him smile. I nod. The knot in my throat makes it difficult to speak.

Sean holds me like that for a moment and then asks, "May I ask why that particular action is off limits?"

I feel him breathing against my back. Sean's pressed his body against my back and holds me tight. "Only if I can ask what you originally wanted this weekend." I glance at him.

"Ah, then it seems we are at an impasse." Those glittering blue eyes conceal his thoughts.

I nod. Damn straight. I'm not spilling my guts if he won't spill his.

Sean's voice is deep and rich. "I suspect the reason, but assumptions usually don't turn out well."

"Are you calling me an ass?" The corners of my mouth tug up. Seriously? What's with him?

Sean laughs like he has no idea what I'm talking about, and turns me towards him. "What?" The smile reaches his eyes.

"You know what happens when you assume, don't you?"

Cocking an eyebrow at me, he tilts his head and tuts, "Grade school humor? Really? Is that what this night has deteriorated into?" Sean shakes his head and sits back down, slumping back into the seat.

I shrug my shoulders and step toward him. "It might be different if you told me what you wanted. I might want that, too." I cross my ankles and gaze at him. Whatever plans he had for the night were blasted to bits when I walked through the door.

Darkness drifts across Sean's eyes, like he's remembering something that he wants to forget. It changes his confident stance and his shoulders slump a little bit. His chest tightens along with his throat. The muscles strain as he tries not to react. I didn't mean to do that to him. I know it's from what I said. I feel horrible about it and want to take away the pain in his eyes.

I walk toward him, not having a plan, just doing whatever feels right. "Sean," I say softly. When he doesn't look up, I put a hand on his shoulder. Still no reaction. I lift one leg gingerly and straddle his lap. That gets his attention. His eyes flick up to mine. A warning shoots through me, but I ignore it. There's something dangerous about him, I can sense it.

I'm standing over Sean and slowly lower myself until I'm on his lap, facing him. I rest my wrists at the back of his neck and look into his eyes.

Sean doesn't move. He doesn't say anything. I tangle my fingers in the curls at the base of his neck and lean in close. Heart pounding, I press my lips to his cheek. I repeat the action, and do it again and again, until I reach his neck. My stomach twists as the space between my legs grows hotter. I tilt my hips, and try to shift my weight on his lap, but Sean stops me.

Watching my face, Sean takes both of his hands and slips them under the hem of my dress. His hot palms run over the outsides of my thighs until they rest on the curve of my butt. Sean holds me tight, and pulls me higher onto his lap. That's when I feel his hard length through his pants. I gasp and dig my fingers into his shoulders.

Sean doesn't smile. Instead, I have the Sean from downstairs, the one who's all dark with no light in his eyes. His fingers press into my skin and he skims the edge of my lace panties.

Neither of us speaks. Sean watches me, always keeping his gaze on my lips as he tilts our hips making his erection rub against my thin panties. I can't hide how much I like it. Cupping my ass, he pulls me against him and then I push back. I'm writhing in his lap, my eyes locked with his. My body aches for his touch. I'm not satisfied with his hands on my bottom. I want them on my breasts; I want them all over me; inside me. I lean my head back and rock against him. Arching my back makes my breasts press against my bra. I moan out loud, and his name slips from my mouth.

That is the action that undoes him. Sean stands suddenly, taking me with him. "Wrap your legs around me," he says as he stands and walks across the room.

The spot between my legs is pressed against him as he walks us to the bed. His gaze doesn't change. The heat in his eyes says that he'll devour me. I wonder what he'll do. Sean leans me back on the bed and looks down at me. "Tell me what you want," he says, climbing onto the bed and laying next to me. His hand strokes my cheek.

"You," I say breathy, "I want to be with you."

Sean's eyes slip over my body after he pushes himself up onto his side. "Tell me when to stop."

I nod. Apprehension shoots through my veins, but lust is boiling hotter. Sean's hands are on me and my eyes close. My back arches into his hand, wanting to feel his touch. Sean starts at my neck, his finger slowly drawing a line down the side of my throat, across my collarbone, and between my breasts. The movement is painfully slow, teasing and igniting heat that surges through my body.

Lightly, his finger traces the swell of my breasts and circles back between them, stopping at my navel. Sean's finger dips in the small indent and continues down, over my dress, and doesn't stop. I gasp when that light touch reaches the dip between my legs. Sean's eyes are locked on mine as his finger trails between my thighs.

I can't look away from his face. I feel trapped, even though I know I can tell him to stop. Sean's hand returns to my face, and this time when Sean trails it down my neck, his fingers remain on my skin. The violet dress has a low neckline, and Sean dips his finger beneath the luxurious fabric, tracing the swell of my breast with his finger.

I breathe harder, wanting him there, wishing he'd do things to me that I never thought I'd want. My nipples harden and press against the lace bra. An image of Sean's teeth, gently tugging the sensitive skin flashes in my mind. I gasp and thrust my chest up toward him, but he doesn't touch me like that. Everything is light, like a snowflake touching skin. His other hand mirrors the movement, tracing the smooth flesh along my neck and down to my breast. By the time he's finished both sides, I'm writhing on the bed. Every bit of me is hot. I've never wanted a man so much. I don't know what to do. My instincts say to pull his lips to mine, but I can't.

Instead, I grab hold of his shirt and yank him toward me. I sit up off the bed and strip his shirt, fumbling the buttons one at a time until they come undone. Sean lets me undress him without saying a word. When I have his shirt off, I nearly die. Every inch of him is ripped, like movie-star-omfg-ripped. The tanned skin is smooth and taut. Muscles rise and fall in perfection. Sean's body is Greek God material. I stare and reach for him, but Sean's hand darts out and he takes my wrist, stopping me.

Shaking his head, he says, "No touching."

Disappointment floods through me and I feel my bottom lip go into a full pout before I realize what I'm doing. "But, why?"

Sean smiles wickedly and leans toward me. His eyes fixate on my mouth. "Pull that lip back in right now or I swear to God, I'll kiss you so hard that you come."

His words shock me. My lip returns to its normal position, but the place between my legs throbs at his suggestion. My eyes lock with his and I feel the surprised, hopeful look fill my face. Heart racing hard, I say, "Can you really do that?"

My only answer is a wicked grin. Before I can say anything else, Sean sits me up. His hands reach for my sides and he starts to slowly unzip the dress. The way he watches me makes me feel excited and uneasy at the same time. I'm perfectly still, trying not to react. Even though I said no kisses, I can't stop looking at his mouth. Images flash through my mind of a kiss that could make me come.

Sean must see it on my face, because he smiles at me. "Just ask, Miss Smith."

I grin at him in return, as his hand slips inside the dress, feeling the smooth curve of my waist. "Don't hold your breath, Mr. Jones."

Mirth flashes in his eyes, and my dress disappears. I'm lying on the bed, propped up on my elbows in nothing but my lingerie. Sean is kneeling on the bed next to me. He drinks in my body like he can't get enough. First his eyes sear across my breasts, and then dip down to my waist, before his gaze lingers on my panties. I try to be calm and confident, the way Miss Black told me to behave, but I can't.

I smile at him shyly and look away. Something inside me wants to cover my body so he can't see me. Sean's finger resumes its slow tracing. When the pad of his index finger slips over my nipple, I can't stand it anymore. I grab him by the wrist. "If you don't touch me, and I mean take me in your arms and press your hands over every inch of my body, I'm going to scream."

Sean grins at me. He leans in close—his lips are next to my ear—and answers, "Will you scream my name, because I'd like to hear that." Before I can answer, Sean presses his lips to my throat, takes me in his arms, and lays me back on the bed. Sean's body is on top of mine. I feel his hard length pressing against me.

That hard body is all mine. My fingers rake down his back as he kisses my neck. The edges of my vision flicker. When I close my eyes, white bursts of light appear. The throbbing between my legs connects to every kiss. Slowly, my legs part and I want him there.

That's when the night goes to hell. In a matter of moments, everything goes from complete ecstasy to complete crap. I hear a high pitched chirping sound coming from across the room. Sean looks up at the same time I do. Neither of us recognizes the sound.

Sean asks, "Is that your cell?"

Shaking my head, I answer, "No. My phone doesn't make that noise." And I have no idea what does.

Sean stands and leaves me lying on the bed. I turn on my side as he walks toward the windows, toward the noise. He presses his hands against the glass and looks down. "Fuck."

CHAPTER 3

"What is it?"

Before he can answer there is a knock at the door. Sean turns in time to see the door open, and drops the black box back into my purse.

Miss Black stands flanked between two large men. They're dresses like hotel patrons in expensive suits, like they might have come to the hotel for a business dinner. They must be the kickass ninjas that Mel mentioned.

Miss Black steps into the room. I take the bedspread in my hands and cover myself. "Mr. Ferro, I believe you're in violation of your contract." She doesn't even look at me when she steps across the threshold. "Get dressed Miss Stanz. You're leaving."

I don't understand what's happening. When I don't move, Miss Black waives a hand at one of the large bald men flanking her. The one with dark skin and inky eyes steps toward me. He picks up my dress from the floor and hands it to me. "Dress yourself, Miss Stanz, or I'll have him do it for you."

Sean leans against the ledge of the window frame with his arms folded over his chest. He looks pissed. "Mind telling me which rule was violated?"

"You know very well which rule, Mr. Ferro." Miss Black looks down at her dress, like she's looking for a piece of lint. She smooths the skirt and glances at me as I pull my dress over my head. I have no idea what she's thinking, or what we did, but here she is.

"Humor me," Sean replies. The look in his eye says he's not happy. The muscle in his jaw works, while he waits.

Black looks him over, with her little brow pinched. "Very well. You took our property off premises. We don't do three strikes here, Mr. Ferro. You were careless and you know, as well as I do, what happens to careless clients in this business."

Sean walks toward her slowly, "I am well aware, however, the violation was an oversight. Miss Stanz followed me outside."

"Why would you do that?" Miss Black's gaze slips from Sean's to mine. I stare at her, heart racing, knowing that I'm going to be busted. Sean can get another virgin to screw, and I'll get kicked to the curb.

I open my mouth to confess, but Sean cuts me off. "Because I asked her to."

"Mr. Ferro, rules are set in stone. We cannot have clients disregarding them. The rules aren't guidelines, they are mandatory. I'm afraid that you'll need to seek your needs elsewhere." Miss Black snaps her fingers at me. "Come, Miss Stanz." Miss Black turns on her heel and walks through the door. I glance helplessly at Sean. He inclines his head slightly, telling me to go. I grab my purse and follow Miss Black out. The two large men are behind me.

Miss Black's long strides are quick. I hurry to keep up. "What happened?" I ask as the elevator doors close. We're alone.

She sighs, like she's annoyed. "He really told you to go outside?" I nod, sticking to the story. "She presses her manicured fingers to her temple. "Men like that are nothing but trouble, always pushing the limits to see how much they can get away with. I'm sorry for putting your through that, Avery. It won't happen again."

"I don't understand how you knew. We didn't go very far. And what was that beeping sound?"

"There's a transmitter in your bracelet." She glances at my wrist. "I already told you that. We know exactly where you are. Where is it?"

"I put it on my ankle." I point and it's still there. "It didn't fit around my wrist."

Miss Black acts like I'm a first grader. "Wrist, Avery—it has to be on your wrist. I'll have it resized." She shakes her head like I'm an idiot.

"I'm sorry. I didn't know."

"Well, you wouldn't. You just started. The beeping noise was a pager we put in your purse." She takes my bag and opens it, taking out a little black box. "It goes off when we are outside the building. That only happens if a client violates their contract. It lets you know that we're coming. I don't normally show up at all, but with you being new, I didn't think you'd leave willingly with the security personnel."

I nod and look at my purse, wondering when she put that inside. I thought I had my bag with me all night. Sean must have seen the pager when he walked over to the window. My purse has an open top and was laying right next to the window. I wonder how he knew what it meant. Sean seemed to know that Miss Black was coming. "Has he done this before?"

Miss Black looks at me, confused. The elevator slows as we reach the ground floor. When the doors open, she resumes her hastened pace. Looking over her shoulder at me, she says, "No, not that I know of. He was a new client."

A car is waiting for us at the curb. Miss Black walks toward it with her head held high. A valet holds the door open for her and she slips into the car. I follow behind her. The men that had entered Sean's room with Miss Black are gone. I don't see them anywhere.

"Stop looking, dear. They're invisible when they need to be." Miss Black slinks back into the seat. Her brow is furrowed and her eyes are pressed closed. "How far did you get? Tell me that you're still a virgin, please." Miss Black looks straight ahead. I'm sitting next to her on the limo seat.

"We didn't get that far. And yes, I am." And I'm not happy about it either. Or maybe I am. I don't know. Tonight was nothing like I thought it would be.

"Good," Miss Black says relieved. "You will be paid for your services for this evening. Mr.

Ferro was required to pay in advance for this evening. So, you don't need to worry about getting stiffed."

"Bad pun."

She laughs and looks at me. I'm staring straight ahead, shell shocked. "You're an amusing girl."

"That's one word for it," I mutter. Glancing at her, I say, "I'm sorry. I feel a little nuts. I thought I was going to—"

She cuts me off. "I know. This job can be an emotional rollercoaster. Don't worry though. It gets easier."

I doubt it, although I say nothing. We arrive back at Miss Black's. I step out of the limo. Before I can walk away, Miss Black says, "I'll find you another client by next weekend. This won't be for nothing. I promise. Come up and let's get this squared away."

I nod, and silently follow her upstairs. I'm paid an insane amount of money, in cash. It isn't anywhere near what I thought I'd be getting, but it is enough to get me through a few weeks, as long as nothing else goes wrong. I take my money and shove it in my purse and head to my car.

After I spray the engine, it starts right up. I drive back to the dorm shivering, with wintry wind blasting my face. I considered sealing the window with duct tape, but that'll look even more ghetto.

When I get inside the dorm, I bypass my room for the moment and go to find Mel. Her door is cracked. It's a little after midnight. I wrap my knuckles on the wooden door and push it open. "Mel? You here?"

Her roommate, Asia, is sitting on her bed talking on the phone. She shakes her head at me, shaking that short shiny black hair. "One sec," she says to the person on the phone. Raising her voice, Asia says to me, "Mel is working late tonight. She said she wouldn't be in until after 2:00am."

I nod. "Thanks."

Flustered, I walk back to my room. If Amber barricaded the door, I'm going to kill her. I slip the key into the lock and twist. Surprisingly, the door opens. My shabby little room is empty. Thank God! As soon as I know that I'm alone, the tears come and they don't stop until I pass out on my bed.

CHAPTER 4

The next morning sucks. Amber and Dennis are arguing. I cover my head with a pillow, but it still doesn't block them out. To top it off, she has the heat cranked up so high that I'm sweating. I get up and turn down the heater. Hiding under the blankets doesn't work when the room is 150 degrees.

"Don't touch that!" Amber snaps at me. "It's freezing in here."

"I'm melting, Amber. Leave it off for a while." I sound reasonable, but she makes a face at me. As soon as I walk away, Amber turns the thing back on.

She turns her anger on me. "You're such a bitch, Avery. You can't do whatever you want, whenever you want. I live here too!" Amber is seething, like she's justified. Dennis watches her, but his eyes flick to me when I explode.

I round on her, growling, with my hands balled into fists at my sides. "Are you fucking insane? I never get to do what I want! You're here all the time, you lock the door, you block me out of my own goddamn room, you have sex on my bed when I'm not here, your boyfriends use my blankets to clean up after they stick their dick in your nasty self! If anyone's a bitch, it's you!" Amber is staring at me, her eyes becoming glossy like she's going to cry. I don't care. I so don't care.

"You're so mean, Avery," Amber sobs and turns to Dennis, who holds her in his arms loosely.

Dennis listened to my little rant. It's quiet for a second before he asks her, "What did she mean, *boyfriends*?" He emphasizes the plural part of the word. "I thought we were exclusive, Amber? Have you been fucking other guys?" He pulls her away and shouts in her face.

I'm so angry. I grab my clothes and run out the door. As it slams behind me, I hear Amber sobbing, saying nasty stuff about me, denying that she was with anyone else. I don't know why he would care. Dennis screws any girl that lifts her skirt. Enraged, I walk down to Mel's and knock. It's still early.

The door creaks open and she looks at me with bleary eyes, "Awh, hell. You want me to go punch Tramperella in the face? Cuz I'll be all over that piece of trash. You just say the word. I could hear you guys screaming from here." Mel yawns the last part and glances down the hall. When I don't answer, she blinks hard and pushes past me. "I'm gonna go all ninja on her white ass. You come on and watch."

I grab Mel's arm and stop her. "Maybe later." Mel looks at me and then back down the hall. I coax her. "Let me use your shower and I'll take you out for breakfast."

Mel gives me a look that's distinctly Mel. It's all attitude. "I want chocolate chip pancakes, and not that shit the diner serves. Are we talking IHOP?"

I laugh. "Yeah, if that's what it takes."

CHAPTER 5

Bribery is underrated. I think I could get Amber whacked if I bribed Mel with a stack of chocolate chip pancakes. She eats them, doused in strawberry syrup. The pancakes look like they've been shot.

"How can you eat that?" I ask. It's so sweet. I have eggs and bacon. Well, I had bacon. Mel took that already.

"It's freakin fantabulous. Everyone should eat this for breakfast. Every day. It's the breakfast of champions." She shovels another bunch of fluffy pancakes into her mouth. A bead of syrup runs from the corner of her mouth.

"That's Wheaties. And you're looking a little vampy, there." I touch to corner of my mouth and tilt my head toward her and say, "You've got syrup. Or is that drool?"

Mel's back stiffens as she wipes away the blot of red. She points a fork full of pancakes at me and says, "I do not drool. Not unless it's a particularly hot guy. Then I might drool, a little." She chews and takes a swig of milk, then asks, "So, how'd last night go? Are we still on Team V?"

I laugh. "You're so stupid. Team V. Yeah, I'm still on Team V. Things got out of hand last night. Black showed up and pulled me away."

Mel's jaw drops and the fork freezes half way to her mouth. "No shit!" She leans in closer and lowers her voice, "What the hell happened?"

I tell her. As I retell the horrible events of last night, I push around the food on my plate. I don't feel very hungry today. When I finish my story, I look up at her. Mel hasn't taken a bite. I tell her, "Black said she'd match me to someone else. I got paid a little bit, enough to treat you and pay some bills, but not enough to be home-free the way I thought I'd be. I don't know what to do."

"You're back to square one."

I nod. "Yeah, I suppose so."

"Why did Sean do that? It almost seems like he wanted to blow the whole arrangement."

"He didn't. He didn't react well when I showed up. He left. I chased him. It's not like he lured me outside to irritate Black. He seemed as surprised as I was when she showed up."

"That boy is messed up." She points her pancake at me before popping it into her mouth.

"We already knew that." I sigh and lean my head on my hand. I poke my eggs and paint the yellow yolk across the white plate.

Mel watches me. "You seem out of it. If I didn't know better, I'd think you were falling for the guy. You're all doe-eyed, making hearts in your food."

"I am not," I say, straightening up.

"Whatever," Mel says, "I just call it like I see it. You've got that Bambi look on your face, like you're swooning for Mr. Freakshow."

I snort-laugh. "You're so mental. That's not it. I just don't know if can do it again."

"It's just one guy, one time," she reminds me.

I nod. "That's what it was supposed to be this time."

————

After breakfast, I head to the library to get caught up on school work. The building is huge and smells like dust and old paper. Once I get into the stacks, the lighting sucks. I navigate my way through the massive building until I find my little chair in the corner. It's a good spot because no one ever comes back here. There's a desk and chair against the wall at the end of one of the rows. I toss my book bag on it and pull out my work.

After a few hours pass, I'm leaning with my hand in my hair, staring at the cinderblock wall in front of me. I can't concentrate. I have no idea what to do. I thought my financial problems were solved and that I could go back to studying. Sean was ideal bait, but then Black sent him packing. I don't know if I can do it with someone else.

Memories flit through my mind and I can feel Sean's hands on my skin. I wish Black hadn't shown up. I wish things progressed further. I wonder what it would feel like to have my sweat-covered body slip over his, what he would feel like inside of me. My body warms at the thought.

I'm so out of it that I don't hear Marty until he's next to me. "Well, looky what we have here."

I jump out of my skin when he speaks and twist in my chair. I had no idea he was there. Marty laughs at me. He's wearing a pair of dark jeans with frayed patches on the thighs, coupled with a tee shirt and denim jacket. His blonde hair is spiked. He looks like an 80's remnant.

I swat at Marty, meaning to slap his leg, but he dodges my hand. "You scared me to death!" I whisper yell at him.

He laughs and drops his backpack on the floor next to my desk, and then takes his extra tall body and leans against the wall. Shoving his hands in his pockets, he says, "Only people with something to hide get all skittish like that. What'd you do? Kiss a girl?" He winks at me and grins.

I cover my heart with my hand, willing it to resume a normal pace, but it ignores me. I don't look at Marty when he speaks and he catches on. "So, you do have something to hide. Is it juicy?" I glance at him, thinking that direct eye contact will help, but the guy sees right through me. In a hushed voice, he squeals, "Oh my God! You have to tell me!" As Marty talks, he falls to his knees and scoots toward me, clutching his hands under his chin, like he's begging.

I laugh it off. "There's nothing to tell." I squirm in my chair and go back to reading my textbook.

"You're a bad liar."

Sighing, I say, "I know," and slump forward, planting my face in the book. "I can't lie, but I can't tell you."

He grabs my shoulder and pulls me up. I look him in the face as he asks, excitedly, "Is this about the questions you asked the other day?" My face must answer for me, because Marty gets more excited. "Oh my God, you did something morally deplorable, didn't you? What was it?"

When I don't answer, he starts reasoning it out, which scares me to death. He ticks off his fingers, "Well, we both know it's nothing to do with lying. So that leaves cheating," he ticks off a second finger and pauses, looking at my slumped shoulders, and says, "Yeah, I can't see that one either. You're hardwired to not cheat. That leaves stealing, adultery—"

"Are you just going to list the seven deadly sins and hope I confess when you hit mine?"

He waves a finger in my face. "Ah ha! That means it was one of the big seven."

"You're an ass. Leave me alone." I pretend to read my book. Marty grabs the pages and yanks it away. "Hey!"

"You tell me everything, why can't you tell me this?" he says holding my book just out of reach. I make a grab for it and miss. He's too damn tall.

"Because I can't. And it doesn't matter now anyway, because everything is all fucked up." I stop jumping for my book and sit down hard in the chair. It feels like a wave of hopelessness crashes into me. Suddenly, I can't breathe and my heart is pounding. I grab the hair on the sides of my head and look at the floor, saying, "I can't do this." My breathing becomes labored, like I'm having an asthma attack.

Marty puts my books down and kneels next to me, placing his hand on my back. "Whoa, Avery. Calm down. Slow your breathing."

Tears well up behind my eyes, but they won't fall. For once, I wish they would. I wish I could just cry and have this part of my life over with. I rock in the seat. "I can't do this."

"Do what, honey? Be more specific." Marty's hand rubs small circles on my back. He leans closer to me. "Tell me, love. I'll help you however I can."

"But that's just it," I look up at him with glassy eyes. "You can't help me, no one can. I have to do something that I don't want to do.

I'm fucked every way 'til Tuesday with no way out."

Marty keeps his hand on my shoulder and looks at me with an expression that I can't read. It's not pity, it's something else, more like pity's bastard cousin. "Avery, you ever think that you're alone because you want to be?" I bristle at the suggestion, but he presses a finger to my lips to shut me up, and shakes his head. "No, don't talk. Listen. There's a time for listening, and that's now. I know you've got no one and that you're all by yourself, but you don't have to be. I'm here and so is Mel. You shut us out, Avery. When things get hard, you retreat into yourself and no one can get through those walls you put up. It doesn't have to be that way. Friends are your family now. I know that I'd do anything for you, you don't even have to ask."

Awh fuck. His words trigger the tears and they rush down my face. Marty smiles at me, like he knows better. Maybe he does. Maybe I'm the one who's fucked up. Maybe I don't have to do everything by myself, but I don't know what that world looks like. The only people that I could depend on through thick and thin were my parents. Family was everything to them, to me. Now that I don't have one, I feel lost, like I don't belong anywhere, like I can't fully trust anyone.

I wipe the tears from my face with the back of my hand.

Marty reaches into his pocket and hands me a clean, white hanky. It's perfectly folded into quarters and creased like he ironed it. He holds it out to me.

I laugh, half choking on the phlegm in my throat. I take the hanky and dab my eyes before wiping my nose. "You made me cry. No one makes me cry."

"Really?" he asks wryly. "Everything makes me cry. Why do you think I walk around with a hanky?" He grins at me.

I look down at the white cloth in my hands, damp with tears. The confession spills out of my mouth. "I was offered a position as a high dollar call girl. If I take it, it solves my money problems. I can finish school and move on with my life."

"But..." he prompts, assuming nothing. Marty's great like that. He doesn't condemn me.

"But the obvious. But I'd be selling my body. But I'd be letting some stranger have sex with me. But, I'd be giving away my virginity to some freak..." my voice fades as I say the word, thinking of Sean.

Marty smiles softly and adds, "But you like someone else."

I look up at him. "How'd you know?"

He shrugs, "Just a hunch. Something about the way your voice sounds, like there's more there than you're saying. So who is this guy?"

I look at my hands as I speak. "No one. I don't even know. He helped me when my car got jacked. I've seen him a few times, and then I got the job offer. After talking to you the other day, I took it… I took the job because he was the client. Then, things got messed up, and now I can't have him." My voice hitches in my throat as I speak. Shaking my head, I ask, "What's wrong with me? How can I like a guy who's that twisted? He ordered a virgin call girl."

"And you showed up," Marty says, patting my knee. "Listen, life doesn't always make sense. Maybe this whole thing's fate, maybe you're supposed to be with this guy in the end—I don't know—but it seems to me that's what's holding you back."

"What is?"

"That fucked up guy. You're totally sure that there is no way for him to be a client again?"

My eyes flick to his. I shake my head. "No, the madam was really pissed."

"Then, raise the stakes. Tell her that it's him or nothing."

"And what if she says no?" I'm screwed if she says no.

"Then, you're no worse off than you are now. Why not try to get the money and the man? Go for the gold, girlie. You're only young once." He bumps his shoulder into mine and smiles at me.

"Got any more clichés that you're dying to use?"

"Nah, I just know how much they irritate you. Go find your boss, call girl. And if you work things out, I'm taking you shopping." Marty gets a giddy look in his eye. "I saw this perfect little dress at Black Label. Any guy would love to rip it right off of you."

I laugh and lean into his shoulder. The whole in the center of my chest, that painful ache that was consuming me, withers and I feel like maybe I can do this. I have to convince Miss Black to get Sean back. I can do that.

I think.

CHAPTER 6

After promising Marty that we'd go shopping tonight, I head to my car. Pulling the seat forward, I toss my books in the back. When I go to push the seat forward, it won't move. It's not as cold today, but still—standing in a parking lot alone is asking for trouble. My track record for getting robbed is shamefully high. I yank the seat, but it's stuck. I climb in the backseat and put all my weight into it and pull, trying to force it into an upright position. There's a cracking sound and then seat comes free and falls back into place. I try to squeeze between the seat and the door so that it doesn't get stuck again, but I don't fit. So, I'm forced to climb through the bucket seats, head first, and I pretty much fall out the door. I stand, brush myself off, and jump into the car. I lean back before grabbing the seatbelt. The crappy old seat holds. I half expected it to snap off.

I start my magic car and head toward Miss Black's. When I arrive, the place is bustling with people. I've never seen anyone here before. There are workers at desks. I hear a woman talking on a phone saying something about insurance for employees. Shocked, I stand there in the door way to the office with my mouth hanging open. It takes this many people to run a brothel? The phones ring nonstop. It's like the call girl call center.

Miss Black spots me from across the room. She's standing at an aged man's desk, handing him a file. An irritated look flashes in her eyes and she quickly walks toward me in her tailored suit. She tucks the remaining files under her arm. "May I help you?"

Nodding, I look at her. "Yes, I believe so."

"Very well, come with me." Miss Black has perfect posture, even in those heels. She walks in front of me and I follow her back to her office, where she closes the door. "It is extremely unprofessional to arrive unannounced, Avery."

"I'm sorry," I say taking a chair. I sit on the edge of my seat and place my hands on her desk. Miss Black is leaning back in her seat, legs crossed. "I needed to discuss something with you."

"I'll allow it this time, however, in the future, if you want to speak with me, it has to wait until you check in on the weekend."

"That's just it. Since things got messed up the other night, I wouldn't be checking in and I didn't want to wait for you to call me. I decided that I'm not cut out for this." My heart is pounding as I speak. I try so hard to keep my nerves off my face. My hands rest perfectly still on her desk. There is no tremor in my voice. "I'm withdrawing my application. Thank you." I stand, like I'm going to walk away.

Her little speech about what a rare commodity I am is my only card to play. I'm totally bluffing. I need this job, but I want it on my terms. I step towards the door and reach for the knob. Miss Black doesn't say anything until I'm ready to pull the door open.

"Wait," she says. I stop and turn to look at her. "Please sit." Miss Black straightens in her chair and leans forward, her eyes tracking me as I walk back toward her and sit down. "The other night was an anomaly. That is not the usual course of events. In all my time doing this, that is only the second time I've had to intervene. I apologize that it made you question your choice to work here. There are other clients who have been on our roster longer, that have a proven track record. I would—"

I cut her off, "I'm not interested. The thing is, I didn't feel threatened the other night and while it might have broken your rules, he didn't make me feel like a prostitute. I didn't expect that to happen. I was the idiot who followed him outside. He wasn't the one who broke the rule. I did."

Miss Black looks at me with her dark eyes. The tips of her fingers press together one by one as she watches me from behind her desk. "You're not telling me something. What is it?"

"I'll consider staying, if I was given a second chance with that client. I won't leave the hotel this time. I'll do my job, and you'll get your money." My throat tightens as I speak. My heart is racing so fast. This scares the hell out of me. The whole thing, and here I am telling her what to do. For all I know, she has those beefcake ninjas locked in her closet and they'll bust out and break my face for suggesting such a thing.

Miss Black stares at me. I don't breathe. My tongue is between my teeth to keep me from spewing her with nervous chatter. Her index fingers press together and then she taps them three times, like she's deciding something. "So, this is about money?"

No. "Yes."

"And..." she prompts.

"And I didn't think I could do this, but after the other night, I know I could follow through with him."

"Even if I wanted to, I don't think I could get him back. We exchanged some terse words after the event." Miss Black taps her desk. She glances up at me.

I rush out what I wanted to say. "Just tell him. If he refuses, then I'll consider someone else. Are we agreed?"

Miss Black isn't stupid. She leans toward me and says, "Something else is going on here, of that I'm certain. However, I'm not one to blow a business deal over suspicion. I'll ask him, under the condition that if he says no, that you'll continue working for us—that you'll trust my judgment when I select another match for you."

I didn't want this part. I suck at lying. I can't just yes her, she'll see it in my eyes. My stomach twists as I extend my hand toward her. "Deal," I say, and we shake on it.

I agreed to be with another man if Sean won't have me.

I hope to God that he says yes.

CHAPTER 7

"No freakin' way is she wearing that dress," Marty says with his hands folded over his chest. He towers over Mel, who is sitting next to him in the middle of a swank shop. Either way, I need a dress for my next tryst. I'm still waiting to hear back if it will be with Sean or not. My stomach is twisting in knots. I don't feel like shopping, but I had hoped that it would distract me. Since Mel and Marty disagree on everything, it's been an interesting evening.

"How can you say that?" Mel says exasperated. This is the seventh dress, the seventh pair of shoes, the seventh set of accessories that I've put on over the last hour and a half. "Look at how tiny her waist looks in that thing. That is THEE dress."

Marty gets up and stands next to me. I'm on a little riser, standing in front of a mirror. The shop attendant looks at me, but says nothing. Marty points to my hips, "True enough, but it does nothing for this region and her boobs! My God, she looks like she's nursed sixteen children. The braless look is for girls with falsies, not our Avery." Marty gestures at my cleavage in this dress, or lack thereof. I look down. Okay, maybe he's right. "A good dress doesn't sacrifice one asset for another." He snaps his fingers at the attendant. "Next please!"

"You're such a drama queen," I say as I step off the box. I add, "And stop snapping at the girl like she's a labradoodle. She hates you enough already."

He bats his eyes at her. "Sorry love. I just get so excited. You're doing a smashing job. Keep up the good work."

The attendant, Amanda, smiles and nods, but I'm sure she picturing strangling Marty in her mind. "I'll get the next dress you chose. Just leave that one in the dressing room for me and I'll put it back."

I nod and traipse into the dressing room. I unzip the dress and pull the supple fabric over my head before putting it back on the hanger. I'm standing in my undies when my phone buzzes. I wouldn't have heard it if I wasn't in the dressing room. I pick it up and recognize the number. It's Miss Black. Immediately, my heart starts to pound and hope fills my chest.

"Hello?" I say, answering the phone with a swipe of my finger. I'm so excited, so terrified. I want the perfect dress for Sean. I can't wait to hear when our next date will be. Sean made is sound like we'd be seeing a lot of each other.

"Miss Stanz, good evening." Miss Black sounds the same as usual. It's hard to read her emotions. Maybe she doesn't have any. "I've contacted Mr. Ferro and wanted to call and tell you the results of our conversation. As I suspected, he is no longer interested in using our services."

A rush of air leaves my lungs and I sit down hard on the puffy seat inside my dressing room. "You told him that it'd be me?"

"Yes, I did. He was rather adamant that he no longer wishes to pursue the arrangement with you, even after I told him that you requested we call to correct this situation. I'll find you another match. Give me a little time and we'll have you all set. I'll call you when everything is ready. Have a good evening." And then the line goes dead. I stare at my phone. I feel like a hollowed out pumpkin. I put my head between my hands and try to collect myself.

Black's words bounce around in my mind. It isn't for a few moments that I realize what they meant—Sean didn't want me. He rejected me. Worry pinches my face as I wonder what I did. Why would he say no? The other night, everything seemed perfect. I don't understand why he would do this. I thought he liked me.

There's a knock on my door. Amanda's voice makes me jump. "I have your next selection here." She opens the door and hangs the dress on a hook. When she turns to look at me, her smile falls. "Are you all right? You look ill."

"I'm fine," I manage to choke out. Pushing away the feelings bombarding me, I plan to fake my way through the rest of the night. I hand her the dress that made me look flat and pull this one on. It's deep blue with silver stitching along the hem. There's a thin belt at the waist and a neckline that dips into a deep V. The skirt hugs my hips before it flares at the thigh. It's sexy and cute, all in one dress.

Zombie-like, I wander into the center of the store and show the dress. There's a fake smile plastered on my face. Mel and Marty both gasp when I walk out. It's a good sign.

Marty speaks first, "That is the dress, like *thee* fuck-me three ways til Tuesday dress."

Amanda blinks, like she's never heard a crass word before.

"Will you shut up, fifty shades of gay, and let her show us the dress!" Mel says to Marty, and hops up to look at me. "Spin around, honey. Show off your stuff." I turn slowly, palms raised while they look me over. "You look hot, Avery. I agree with the drama queen over there. You have to get this one. It's perfect. Sean will love it."

I swallow hard and keep the smile on my face. "It's not for Sean."

"What?" they say in unison.

Marty looks at Amanda and flicks his hand while he talks, "Go get us sparkling waters, honey." Amanda smiles and walks off. No doubt she's going to spit in his. Marty and Mel flank me. We look in the mirror as we talk in hushed voices. "What happened? How do you know?"

"I got a call while I was in the dressing room. Sean declined."

Mel's eyes go wide and she looks at Marty who is uncharacteristically silent. Mel takes over. She slips her hand around my waist and says, "To hell with him, then. You don't need him,

Avery. He was eye candy. A crush. Nothing more. I'll help you pick out a new guy, someone better."

Marty eyes her. "You too? Is the whole school whoring, now?"

Mel goes on the defense. She folds her arms over her chest and narrows her eyes. "You got a problem with that?"

"No," Marty says, almost whining, "I feel left out."

That makes me laugh. It caught Mel off guard too and she snorts so loud that she sounds like a pig. We both stare at her. "Like you expected him to say that?" I shake my head. "Where'd you find this basket of gay, anyway?"

"He's my lab partner," I respond, waiting to see what Marty does about the gay accusation, but he just glosses over it. I wonder what's going through his head. The last time I assumed I knew something about someone from the way they looked, well, it didn't go well. It turns out that the woman wasn't pregnant. Since then, I don't blurt things out like that.

"That was witty," Marty says, pressing his hand to his chin and examining Mel like he's never seen her before. "I like what you did there." The two of them chatter and I look at the dark blue dress and know that some other guy will be taking it off of me. I swallow hard and walk back to the dressing room to take it off. This is the dress that will be on me when I solve my financial problems. This is the dress that some guy will remove from me the night I lose my virginity.

Several hundred dollars later, I'm leaving the swank little shop with a new dress and silk shoes. It cost a good chunk of the money I earned with Sean, but it's necessary to do whoever's next. After we walk outside, I put the things in my car.

"Let's go grab a bite to eat," Marty says.

"Sounds good to me," Mel replies.

Marty claps like he's five and yells, "Shotgun!" This is a major turn of events, since he rode to the store with me. Mel met up with us and brought her car. Glancing at me he says, "No offense hun, but your car scares the glitter out of me."

"None taken," I say. "Listen, I'm going to run an errand and head back. I'm not really hungry, yet. Late lunch." I'm lying, but neither one calls me on it. I wave and duck into my car.

I have to pick up my last paycheck from my previous employer. By the time I get there, it's dark outside. The sun sets so early at this time of year. My sweater doesn't do much to keep the chill away. I need to buy a coat. My mother would have yelled at me for wearing something so thin. God, I miss her. On chilly nights like this, she'd be cooking chicken noodle soup. Bread would have been baking in the oven all day, filling the house with that wonderful aroma. Memories like that sneak up on me at the worst times. I sit in my car for a moment, trying to push the past away.

Moving fast, I jog across the parking lot and walk into the front of the restaurant. There's a line of people waiting to be seated. A man is talking to the hostess. There's a beautiful woman on his arm. She has deep brown hair with a hint of red. A black dress clings to her curvy body. I envy her for a moment, wishing that I had curves like that.

"Hey, Stacy," I say as I approach the hostess. "I just need to pick up my check."

"Sure, but they weren't ready when I came in. You might have to wait for it."

I nod, intending to walk past her. I'm dressed like a bum, with tight jeans and my holey sweater. I stand out like a stripper in a preschool. A chill washes over me as I'm about to pass her. The guy at the podium turns. His blue eyes lock with mine and I freeze in place.

Sean.

We stare at each other for half a beat. Sean's wearing a black suit that fits him so well. It shows off his shoulders and his trim frame. The shirt he's wearing is the color of the night sky, perfectly blue—dark like my new dress. A chill encases my heart, as it tries to climb up my throat. I can't do anything but stare.

The girl on his arm, leans in close, possessively. "Is there a problem?" she snaps.

I blink and shake my head. I hate her. I hate everything about her. I want to rip her face off. My fingers flex at my sides as I think about it, but I'd rather Sean didn't know how hung up I am on him. "No ma'am," I say, knowing ma'am pisses off anyone under thirty years old. "Your table will be ready in a moment."

I shoulder my way past them, leaving Sean staring after me.

I get to the back room and find Lenny's office. He's my boss, or he was until Miss Black stole me away. "Hey," I say, my heart still racing from seeing Sean. "Is my check ready?"

"Yeah. I just finished. Here it is. I hope you come back, if you ever need a job again. You're a good kid." Lenny hands me my check. He's an older guy with gray stubble on his face. His white hair is thin and flops to one side. He reminds me of my dad when he isn't screaming at the staff.

I nod, fingering the check. "I will. Thanks for everything."

"No problem, Avery."

I smile at him and leave the office. I head through the kitchen and get enough dirty looks to last a lifetime, but I have to get to the back door. There is no way I'm leaving through the front. I'm lucky I maintained my composure the first time. If I see Sean again, I'll go nuts.

I leave through the receiving door and walk around the parking lot, back to my car. The parking lot is well lit, but there are still patches of shadow. I eye my car and hurry, walking fast, rubbing my arms to try and keep warm. A jacket is definitely a priority. When I get to my car, I stuff my check in the glove box and grab a can of ether. I lift the hood and hold it up while I spray, holding my breath so that I don't breathe it in.

"Miss Smith," a familiar voice says behind me.

CHAPTER 8

"It's a wonderful night for a spray start car," Sean says. Startled, I flinch and the can of ether goes flying. It smacks into my windshield, chipping it, before rolling down into the engine. Sean reaches under the hood and grabs the can. "A bit jumpy, are we?"

"Yes, I am," I say, snatching the can from him, after I drop the hood. "When strange guys come up to me, things never end well." I try to walk past him to get in my car, but he doesn't move. When I look up into his face, I'm angry. "Better get back to your new hooker. She didn't seem like a patient woman, if you ask me."

"I didn't ask you," he says with confidence that I've never felt.

"Real nice. You scared the crap out of me and cracked my windshield. Unless you plan on robbing me, go away." I fold my arms over my chest and look anywhere but at Sean. The parking lot is fairly empty. It's dinner time and the place is packed. It's always packed.

"What would I take? That dress you have in the backseat—"

"Tell me what you want or go away," I say. My nails are biting through my sweater and into my skin. I lock my jaw, trying so hard to keep from saying something stupid.

"Is that dress for your next lover?"

"It's not for you, if that's what you're asking." I'm bristling. I don't mean to. I don't want to, but I can't stop. Sean has my blood pumping and my body just reacts.

Sean's eyes flick over me, like he's amused. "I don't wear dresses, although I appreciate the thought."

"Let me in my car," I hiss and drop my hands to my sides. He's blocking the door.

"What will you do if I say no?" His eyes sparkle, like he thinks this is funny.

I lean in close to his face. A twisted smile snakes across my lips as I speak. "I'll take your nuts off and then run you over with my car."

Sean flinches and steps away from the door. I push past him, brushing his shoulder and fighting the urge to throw myself into his arms. I'm so messed up. He's on a date with a hooker and I still want him. How many times was I dropped on my head as a baby? There's no way that this is normal. I sit down hard in the driver's seat and yank the door shut.

Sean leans on the door, resting his hands on the roof. He speaks into the open window. "You're beautiful when you're angry."

"Go to hell." I turn the key in the ignition and the car backfires and rumbles to life. God, could this be worse? Is he here to taunt me? I don't get it. I throw the car into reverse and rev the engine, ready to peel out, but his words stop me.

"I would have rather had you." Sean straightens and turns to walk away. His hands are in his pockets as he strolls back toward the restaurant.

The car sputters and stalls. I stopped feeding the engine gas without realizing it. I throw the car into park and jump out. "Wait!" Sean stops and turns around to look at me. There's a golden glow on his head from the light above. His hands are in his pockets and there's a faint smile on his lips.

I leave my car where it is and run the three steps toward him. "What do you mean?"

Sean looks me over like I inhaled too many fumes. "You were my preference."

I stare at him like I've been hit in the head with a board. "Then why did you tell her no?"

Something flashes behind his eyes, but it fades quickly. He tries to conceal it by looking down and pushing a rock with his shoe. "I shouldn't have," he confesses.

"Then fix it." Heart beating too hard, I stare at him.

Sean's gaze lifts and meets mine. "I was under the impression that it's not the kind of thing that I could fix."

"If you don't want me, I suppose that I could screw someone else—" I turn from Sean, but he grabs my wrist and pulls me back.

"I never said that I didn't want you." He flips open his phone and dials. I stare at him. Someone picks up. "I've changed my mind," he says without any introduction. "Yes, Miss Stanz. I want her delivered to my doorstep wearing nothing but a bow tomorrow night." He hangs up before the person can respond. His eyes are locked on mine the entire time. "Is that plain enough?"

Giddy hope flutters inside of me. I'm so fucked up. Why do I like this guy? He's on a date with a hooker. He ordered me on the phone. He wants me naked, in a bow.

"Maybe." I try to hide my smile, but suck at it. I rub my arms, trying to chase away the chill.

Sean takes off his jacket and places it over my shoulders. "Come inside and have dinner with us."

All sorts of nervous energy snake through me. I twist my hands and say, "With you and your hooker? I'm not into threesomes. I know it's not on my list yet, but I'm pretty sure I'm not into that."

"How do you know if you haven't tried?" His voice is light, teasing. He grins at me.

"Because I'm possessive. I don't share."

Sean looks down and then up again. The movement makes my stomach feel like it's floating away with my brains. Those dark lashes are delicious. "I like that. I don't share, either. The woman is my accountant. We were going over some records this evening. I didn't think I'd see you again, but I'm glad I did. Come inside."

I shake my head and look back at my car. It's halfway out of the parking spot. "I can't. I mean, I shouldn't. Black would be pissed if she found out about it." *And you act so hot and cold, that I feel like I have whiplash.*

The way his eyes devour me makes me weak. Somehow Sean manages to get close to me. Before I know it, Sean's rubbing his finger over my arm, gently. He looks at me from under his lashes, and says, "Please."

I melt. How can I refuse him? He sees it in my face. I offer up one last halfhearted protest. "But, I'm not dressed for it."

He takes my hand, "I don't care." Sean pulls me to his chest and wraps his arms around me. The way he looks down at me makes me shiver. Desire flames to life inside of me. "I wish I could kiss you." His lips barely brush mine as he speaks. It's a cruel trick, a kiss without kissing.

"Maybe, someday."

This makes him smile.

CHAPTER 9

I sit at the table in my tattered jeans and oversized sweater, feeling out of place. When I look up from my plate, Sean's eyes are on me. He explained to his accountant that I was an old friend and that I'd be joining them for dinner. Her eyes swept over me before giving me a look that said she thought I wasn't a threat. Whatever. She can take her perfect body and shove it. Besides, all Sean's attentions are directed at me.

Dayla has a tablet on the table, where she presses buttons, asking Sean to clarify expenses. "You can't take a deduction on that Sean."

"I wouldn't have come here if the damn merger went through." Sean says, ripping off a piece of bread from the loaf on the table. "The additional trip isn't an expense?"

She sighs, "You're private jet isn't an expense. I need the fuel bill when you get back, along with these other papers." Her eyes flick to me. "Can you believe him? He avoids New York at all costs and then spends money like it's water when he finally gets here."

I have no idea who Sean is, why he's avoiding New York, or the reason for the sudden spending spree. I just smile politely and say, "Yeah, Sean's always pissed away money like a drunk sailor when he hits the Big Apple."

Sean grins at me. Dayla rolls her eyes. "It wouldn't be so bad if he told me what some of these expenses were. Like this one. What cost you $8,000 last weekend?"

Sean's eyes remain amusedly locked on mine. My stomach flutters. "Entertainment," he says.

It takes me a moment, but I realize who he spent that money on. That was the down payment for me. Sean sees the comprehension in my eyes and winks at me when Dayla has her eyes glued to her tablet. Excitement flutters through me and I smile awkwardly.

Dayla looks up and says, "I need more information, Sean. Honestly, how am I supposed to be your accountant if you don't tell me specifics? I need specifics." She glances at me, looking for help.

I lean back in my chair and say, "I'm not getting involved. He's your client. You fix him."

She laughs lightly and gives me an *if only* look. "God bless the woman that brings him to his senses."

Sean doesn't look phased, but his eyes shift between us, like it worries him. He cuts our conversation short. "Unless there are more questions, we need to be on our way."

"Nothing you didn't already *avoid* telling me." Her pretty face pinches as she scrolls through her tablet, shaking her head.

Sean stands and says, "Do the best you can. I don't expect you to find a way to deduct, claim, or mark everything as an expense." She nods slowly, like her mind is still reeling from the meeting. "Please, take your time. I'll take care of the bill."

"Email me a copy," she insists. "This was a working meal."

Sean nods and heads to the front. I don't know why I didn't see him when I was working here. I would have remembered him. "Do you come here a lot?" I ask.

"No, why?" He tells the hostess that he'd like to settle his bill with the waiter. She rushes off to find him. Sean turns back to me, waiting for an answer.

"I worked here, until a few days ago."

He grins at me. "You got a better job, I hear. One with benefits."

I laugh, "Benefits for you, maybe."

"Miss Smith, you dismiss me too quickly. I assure you that this arrangement will benefit both parties." The hostess returns with our waiter. Sean's eyes rake over me, openly admiring my body. I look away, unable to process what's happening. *We just had dinner. That's all. We ate. Pull yourself together, Stanz.*

Sean settles the bill and gives the waiter a big enough tip to render him speechless. His jaw drops as Sean walks away with me on his arm.

The nippy night air blasts me in the face as soon as we're outside. I shiver and try to race toward my car, but Sean grabs my wrist. "Where do you think you're going?"

"Home, lunatic. I'm not supposed to be with you right now."

"Says who?"

"Says you," I say to him, smiling. He's wrapped his arms around my waist and pulls me to him. I mimic his phone call from earlier, "I want her delivered to my doorstep wearing nothing but a bow."

Sean smiles. The way it spreads across his face makes me melt. Oh my god. "I did say that, didn't I?" I nod. "Well, we haven't had dessert."

I twist out of his arms, laughing lightly. "I am not eating dessert with you."

"Who said we'd be eating? You're the dessert," Sean says tugging my arm playfully. "And I can't wait to taste you."

I can't wipe the smile off my face. Laughing, I pull away from him again. "I have to leave. Go eat a KitKat." He follows me across the parking lot to my car. I stop in front of my door, expecting him to try and kiss me, but he doesn't. Sean remains two steps away. "Thanks for dinner."

"My pleasure." There's a look in his eye. It makes me want to be chased.

I open my car door and grab the can of ether. I spray the engine, walk back to my seat, slip in and close the door. Sean is sitting next to me in the passenger seat. "So, dessert."

"Seriously?" I laugh. "This is the car from hell, or have you forgotten?"

"Oh, I have not forgotten. This car is vividly seared into my memory." Sean takes my hand and lifts it to his mouth and presses his lips gently. A light tugging sensation snakes through my body, pulling me toward those lips like they're magnetic. Sean lifts his sapphire eyes and looks at me.

I forget to breathe. I forget everything. I take a jagged breath and pull my hand out of his. "I need to go."

"I'm going with you." Sean takes his seat belt and pulls it across his lap, ready to shove it into place.

"I wouldn't do that."

CHAPTER 10

He does it anyway. The metal clicks and his seatbelt is buckled. "Tell me not to come if you don't want to see me." Sean watches my face as he says it, knowing that I don't want him to leave. He lifts his hand to my face and trails his fingers down my cheek. Images of slippery bodies passes through my mind.

"That's not it." I breathe. He's an inch from my lips. That tugging consumes me. I want to close the distance and press my mouth to his, but I don't.

"Then what is it?" he replies softly.

I'm quiet for a moment. I've forgotten what I'm talking about. His eyes are so beautiful. The curve of those lips is hypnotic. No wonder why I can't think around him. I find my brain and tell him. "That seat belt only buckles. It's doesn't unbuckle."

Sean grins wolfishly, like he just deflowered an entire flock of virgins and I'm next. "I guess I'm going with you, then."

Shaking my head at his tenacity, I start the car. It lurches out of the parking spot and I get onto the road. Sean reaches for the heater. I tell him not to, but it's too late. A puff of white smoke shoots out of the vents. Reaching for the switch, I flip it off. "Don't touch anything."

"There's no heater?" he balks, but when he glances at me, he looks concerned. "Why aren't you ever wearing a coat?"

"Because I don't have one. They're expensive and it seemed like a waste of money. When it's really cold out, I have a sweater I can wear."

"You mean that other oversized ball of yarn I saw you wearing?" I nod. His eyes flick to the window, where it's cracked open next to my head, blasting me with cold air. "Why are you still driving this thing? It's a death trap."

I shoot him an evil look. "Seriously? You're asking me why I'm driving a shitty car? Because, I don't have eight grand to blow whenever I want. I can barely keep this thing running as it is." There must be something about the way I say it, because Sean doesn't press me. Instead the topic shifts to him.

Sean's fingers are at the top of the window, and he looks outside and up at the sky. "I haven't been here at this time of year in a long time. I forgot how much I like it. The air smells like snow." He gives me a half smile and asks, "Where are we going?"

"You'll see." I drive into a park. It's past dark and there aren't many lights along the road once we're inside.

Sean looks around and says, "If I wasn't stuck in my seat, I'd be worried you were going to hack me up and leave me in the woods."

Grinning, I reply, "I have to get you out of the seatbelt somehow."

"You're a little twisted, you know that?"

"Oh, and you aren't?"

"I never said that." Sean gives me a look and shakes his head.

"What then?" I say, driving past the building I was looking for. There are a few cars in the parking lot. I drive around back and stop the car. It shudders and dies.

"You surprise me, that's all." Sean looks around and asks, "Where are we?"

"At the skating rink." I get out of the car and walk around to his side. I yank open the door to find him trying to free himself from the seat. "I'll get it. Wait a second." I flip open the glove box and grab a screwdriver. I lean across his lap and shove the screwdriver into the buckle. I can feel Sean's breath on my cheek. His scent fills my head as I jiggle the screwdriver and the buckle comes free. "There." Sean's gaze is intense, like I just did something so sexy that he's going to die. The way he looks at me, makes every nerve in my body feel like it's strung tight. I want to scream in giddy excitement and laugh.

"Thanks," Sean says, his voice a little too husky. I turn and walk away from the car. Sean steps out of the old car and slams the door. "What are we—?" he asks but doesn't have a chance to finish before getting hit in the face with a snowball.

I laugh hysterically, standing next to the enormous pile of ice shavings from the rink. After they fix the ice, all the shavings are dumped out back to melt. It's the funniest thing to grab some snow and hurl a snowball at someone when it's summer. Since it's cold outside, there is a lot more than normal because it hasn't melted yet, but still—Sean doesn't expect it. The look on his face is priceless.

Sean turns toward me in slow motion, his eyes taking in the pile of snow. "You took me here to have a snowball fight?"

I nod. "Well, I can't exactly take my chastity belt off for just anyone. You have to earn it, man."

"I thought I bought it," he says, walking slowly toward the pile of snow. It's taller than both of us. It looks like the huge snow piles you see in parking lots after the plows push all the snow aside.

I back up the hill, grinning like a lunatic. "You bought the belt, not the key."

"I'm going to pretend that I'm not in metaphorical hell and—"

Smack! I hurl another snowball at him. It hits his cheek and explodes into powder.

"You talk too much," I giggle and start grabbing snow and throwing snowballs as fast as I can.

Sean doesn't hesitate. He runs up the pile of snow in his black suit and tailored black coat. He runs up the hill so that he's higher than me. I nail him in the stomach with a few throws before he has time to retaliate. A snowball clips my ear and the snow goes down my sweater. My hands start to sting from my lack of gloves, but I don't really notice. We're laughing and jumping around on the snow hill, pegging each other like little kids. Sean laughs so much that his eyes water. When I least expect it, he charges me running straight at me. Sean's body collides with mine, and he pins me in the snow, holding my hands down at my sides.

I yelp as snow goes places it shouldn't. "You suck! Let me go! Lemme go! Lemmegahhhh!" My laughter turns into hysterical screeches when he yanks my feet and snow gets shoved up my back. I try to twist away, but he doesn't let me.

Flailing, I kick my legs out of his grip and swing. My leg clotheslines him and Sean falls next to me. I take my chance and jump on top of him, straddling him and shove snow in his face. "You're so mean!" I laugh, trying to make him eat snow.

Sean grabs my wrists and pulls me down on top of him. Our eyes lock and I can't look away. I'm freezing, but I don't care. I want him. Leaning in slowly, I think about kissing him, about how it would feel. That's when someone opens the backdoor to the ice rink and starts yelling.

"You damn kids! Get the hell out of here!" He can't see us, it's so dark, but we've been so loud up until now that he knows we're here. He shines a flashlight at the snow pile.

My eyes go wide and I stifle a laugh. I get off Sean and pull him to his feet, dragging him by the wrist around to the back of the snow pile. We stay there for a second, until the guy gives up, and then burst out laughing.

"Holy shit," he says, doubled over and breathing hard. "I haven't gotten yelled at like that since high school."

"Yeah, what'd you do then?" I say, laughing.

"Toilet papered the principal's car... and got caught by said principal when he left for lunch early." Sean snorts a blast of laughter and shakes his head. "He let me have it."

I smile at him as we head to my car. It feels like I should take his hand in mine, but I don't. We smile at each other and get back into the car. Breathing hard, I look at him. My face is frozen and I've been smiling so much that it's stuck like that.

"Thanks," I say.

"For what?" Sean looks at me, but he doesn't know it yet. There's a stain that mars my life. It hangs over me like a lead balloon.

"I haven't laughed so much in a really long time."

Sean takes my hand and holds it to his lips, cradling my frozen fingers between his. "Neither have I." Sean opens his mouth, like he wants to say more, but he doesn't. Instead he releases my hand and I drive him back to the restaurant where he grabs his bike and we part ways.

CHAPTER 11

By the time I get home, I'm cold and tired. My head is spinning, unable to understand how tonight went from disastrous, to bliss. The laugh lines on my face seem like they're going to be etched onto my skin until I walk into my dorm room. Amber is on top of some guy, riding him like a horse, and they're both naked. I look away, but it's not before I get an eye full of her bouncing boobs and sex noises that I could have lived without hearing. Again.

I go into the shower and lock the door. I stay in there forever, hoping they'll both pull their groin muscles or something. After a while, the hot water beats on my back and I start thinking about Sean. I wonder if I'll ever be like that. Amber's a skank. I wonder what made her that way, and hope to God that it doesn't happen to me. When I get out of the shower, I wrap myself in a towel and pad out into our room. The monkey loving is over, and I head to find clothes.

Amber is sitting up on her bed with a pink sheet draped over her body. The guy she was with is gone. Disgusted, I say, "Was that the fourth guy this week?"

"Yes, no thanks to you. Dennis tried to dump me after you blabbed." Amber grabs a pack of cigarettes and smacks them into her palm after opening the window. She's smoking again. Wonderful.

"There'd be nothing to keep secret if you didn't screw every guy who walked in here." I yank a pair of sweats on and head to my bed.

Amber laughs bitterly, "You need to get laid. You should have taken up what's-his-face up on the three way."

"You disgust me," I say, staring at the ceiling and wishing she'd fall out the window.

"Are you saving yourself, Avery? You think the right guy will just waltz into your life and you'll be in love? Get real. Life doesn't work that way. Sex is dirty. It has nothing to do with love."

"I feel sorry for you," I mutter, not thinking about what I've said.

"Screw you, bitch. You act like you're better than me, but you're not. You're a goddamn whore, you just don't know it yet." She sucks on her cigarette and holds it in. "Or maybe you do and that's why you're such a bitch." She releases a cloud of white smoke out the window.

When people find out that Amber's my roommate, they feel sorry for me. Her reputation precedes her. She's a total whore and everyone knows. The thing is, while she's absolutely vile, her words are true. I turn my back on her and feel the center of my chest cramp. After tomorrow, I'll be a whore—a real one.

Pressing my lips together, I say, "You're right."

Amber laughs, like she doesn't believe me. She waits for me to say something else, to bash her again, but I don't. I can't. I'm a hypocrite. I don't like that she's slutty, because it affects me. No, that's not true. I don't like her because she's vile, because she's always got some guy's dick in her mouth. At least that's what I've told myself all this time.

I don't want to think about it anymore. I close my eyes, willing sleep to come, but it doesn't. I lay there long after Amber passes out.

My heart races so hard that I can't stand it. I curl into a ball and feel the tears streak my face. I wish things weren't the way they are. I fall asleep, wishing my life to be different, hoping for a miracle.

CHAPTER 12

Miss Black calls me and lets me know that I have a date this evening. I wear my new dress. This time I change in my room. Amber isn't around. She's avoiding me, which is kind of nice. I zip my new dress and put my heels in my shoulder bag, since I have to drive my car to Black's.

When I arrive, Miss Black looks me over, approves my dress and then does all the measurements. Lastly, she comments on my lingerie. I'm wearing a white cotton set that's trimmed with embroidery and lace. The bra is no more than a shelf. It barely conceals my nipples.

If I lean forward, I'll fall out of the bra and the dress.

Miss Black says, "The bikini panty is fine for the virgin gig, but when this is over, I want you in a thong or g-string. No exceptions." I feel like a bad employee. I nod and don't say anything. She seems to think that I'll be staying here for a while, even though I told her that I'm not.

"Since the other night didn't go well, I'm changing protocol with you. Here's a phone. I will call you if your bracelet goes off premises. Mr. Ferro gets no more chances, understood?" I nod and she shoos me. "Get dressed and go to the car, and remember—confidence. Even if you have no idea what he wants or what you're doing, act like you do."

I walk to the car that's waiting for me at the curb and climb into the backseat. I've had more time to think about this, so I'm not as nervous. Last time I was near puking. This time I just have a serious case of butterflies. The car pulls up in front of the same hotel. I'm given the same room number, which surprises me. I wonder if this is his room, if this is where he's staying while he's in New York.

Shoulders back, I walk across the lobby to the elevator. I press the button to the penthouse. When the doors open I walk to the end of the hall and knock. Sean pulls the door open. He's wearing a white button down shirt that's open at the neck with a tie that's been undone. The shirt is tucked in at the waist to a pair of tailored slacks. He's barefoot. The stubble on his cheeks makes him sexier than he already is. His eyes slip over me and it feels like a caress.

"I told them naked with a bow, Miss Smith. Do I need to call your employer?" Sean sounds serious, but the smile on his face makes my nerves fade.

I walk past him and into the room. "They said I wasn't allowed to walk naked through the lobby."

"And you do everything you're told?"

"Only sometimes. Maybe." I smile. "I'll try it next time, if you like."

He laughs to himself and shuts the door. Sean walks across the room and closes a laptop that's open on the table. He's been working. There are dark circles under his eyes like he's under a tremendous amount of stress. I didn't notice them last night. I walk further into the room and look around. It's the same as the other night. He must be living here.

Sean crosses the room and grabs a bottle from the bar. "A drink, Miss Smith?"

"No, thank you, Mr. Jones. I'm a professional. We don't drink."

"You're not allowed to drink, are you?" he asks.

"I can. It's not forbidden." He walks toward me with a predatory look in his eye. It makes my stomach twist.

"Then, why not?"

"I don't my first time to be when I was too drunk to remember. Call me romantic, but it sounds more appealing to me that way." I'm nervous. My fingers tug at the fingers on my other hand. I try to stop, but then I just do something else.

Sean's eyes remain fixed on my cleavage. "You're very appealing, so is your notion of remembering." His eyes lift to my face. "Are you expecting to be interrupted this evening?" I shake my head. "Good. Let's begin where we left off last time. Strip. Throw that beautiful dress on the floor and lay on my bed."

My heart is pounding. I didn't think he'd do this. Sean's acting cold, distant. It's like I don't know him. "Are you sure?"

"Yes," he says evenly. "Do it." Sean sits down in the chair and watches me.

My heart is pounding so fast that I can't hide how nervous I am. Maybe I should have taken that drink. I reach for the zipper and slide it down. I shimmy my shoulders out of the dress and it falls to the floor, puddling around my ankles. Sean's hot gaze drinks in my body. When I turn away to walk over to the bed, he stops me.

"Wait." I stop. "Come here." I walk toward him with my heels still on. The bra barely contains me. I stop in front of him.

Sean reaches for me slowly. He places his hands around my back and pulls me closer, and then palms my breasts through the bra. The shock of how he behaves makes me want to cry. He's acting like I'm an object. I don't like this, but I can't stop. Sean doesn't get another chance. And if I say no, this is over.

Sean squeezes my breasts, but it scares me. It doesn't feel like I'm here with him. I have a darker version of the man I lo—

Oh my God. That's when I realize it. I love him. I'm here thinking that this job is going to be something else, but it's not. Sean doesn't have any romantic inclinations toward me. I want to yell at him. I want to slap him in the face and ask how he could behave this way, but I can't.

Sean's eyes cut to mine and for a brief second, I see remorse. It's there and gone faster than I can blink. Sean is cold, detached. He points to the bed. "Go lay down, the way you were the other day." I want him, but I want the guy from the restaurant, the guy from the snowball fight, the one who stopped to help me get my car back. For some reason he's shut down and I don't know how to draw him out. Half way to the bed, I stop and look back at him.

"Do what I tell you," he says.

Heart pounding, I go to the bed and lay in the spot I was in the other day. He watches me, but doesn't move from the chair. "Spread your legs." I do as he says, parting them. My heart thumps wildly in my chest. I don't know if I can do this. I want Sean. I want to crack that shell. "Now slip your hand down your panties and rub, slowly."

I glance at him, feeling shame spreading across my face. "Sean, please…"

"When you've done that, I'll come over." He doesn't move. The stern expression on his face doesn't change.

I can leave or stay. I can protest. Or I can do what he wants. Feeling foolish, I do as he asks. I slip my hand between my legs and rub. At first the only thing I feel is complete foolishness, but my body comes to life. I'm too emotionally charged for nothing to happen. Sean watches me from across the room. Slowly, I relax and just think about the sensations shooting through me.

When I stop looking for him, Sean's next to me. I feel his weight on the bed.

Sean breathes in my ear. "May I?" he asks, slipping his hand on top of mine, lowering it to the sensitive flesh between my legs. I nod and go to pull my hand away, but he holds it there. "You stay," he says as he dips his hand lower and strokes my slick skin. I gasp, surprised at the intensity of the touch. My hips rise up to meet his hand.

My heart is beating so fast, so hard. I feel warm and afraid. I want to relax. I want to be with him, but I'm not his lover. I'm his hooker. Before I realize it, tears are streaking down my cheeks. Sean's hand gently strokes me, but I don't look at him. I can't.

Sean's fingers slip inside of me and I jump. He's been kissing my neck and finally pulls back to look at me. "Avery," he says, his voice filled with concern. Sean takes his hand out of my panties and pulls me to his chest. Cradling me in his arms, he asks, "Why are you crying?"

Shaking my head, I say, "I'm fine. Something got in my eye." Sean nods and takes my wrist, pulling my off the bed. "Where are we going?"

"I want to take a bath with you. Can we do that?" his eyes meet mine, and although I don't understand, I do as he asks.

Nodding, I say, "Yes, that would be nice." I press my lips together and manage to stop the tears.

Sean fills the huge tub in the bathroom and invites me in. The room is blush colored marble, with white accents. It's beautiful. Sean takes my hand and pulls me to him. Wiping the moisture from my cheeks with his hands, he pulls me to him and holds on tight. He whispers in my ear, "I'm sorry. I didn't mean to..." he sighs and pulls back, looking at me. Smiling sadly before glancing at the tub, Sean waves his hand, like I should step in clothed. I nod and step into the warm water. When I sit back, he takes my hand.

Sean smiles at me, but I still feel sick. I must look green because he says, "We don't have to do this."

"Yes, we do. I have to get over it and just do it. Nothing in my life turned out the way I thought it would. Why would this be any different?" I sound bitter. I can't hide it.

Sean sits on the edge of the tub and looks down at me. My white panty set is see through. When his gaze flicks back to my face, he says, "I'm sorry. I didn't mean to look before you're ready, but you're beautiful. I couldn't help myself."

I manage a weak smile. "You weren't acting like yourself." It's a statement, a fact.

His eyes dart to the side, like he's ashamed. "I didn't know how to act."

"I thought you've done this before."

"I have, it's just. This is different," he says, pushing his hands through his hair.

"Why? I don't understand."

"I know you don't Avery. Just believe me when I tell you that it's different. I didn't know the others. I know you. I like you. It changes everything." His voice drops to a whisper and he won't look at me.

I swallow hard, and stand in the water. Water pours off me in sheets as I stand and reach around to unhook my bra. The clasp comes undone and I drop it on the bathroom floor at Sean's feet. He watches me, his eyes darkening by the moment. He looks at my breasts like he wants to lick them. I shimmy out of the wet panties and toss them to him. Sean catches them. A smile flicks across his face.

"A sudden case of exhibitionism, Miss Smith?" he can't seem to pull his gaze up to my face.

I take his hand and pull him to me. His feet are on one side of the tub. I press my naked, wet body against him and drag my fingers through his hair. I decide that I have to do this all the way or not at all. I'm holding back and so is he. I hope that removing my barrier will cause his to come down as well.

Looking into his eyes, I say, "Shut up and kiss me."

CHAPTER 13

Any remaining wall that Sean has up, crumbles and falls. He presses his body tightly against mine before sweeping his lips over mine. The kiss is gentle at first and then becomes more demanding. His tongue sweeps over my lips, demanding that I part them. When I open my mouth, he dips inside. Sean kisses me harder and I love it. My fingers tangle in his hair. The damp shirt clings to his chiseled chest. I press my breasts harder against him, wishing that I could feel his skin against mine. As if he can read my mind, Sean pulls away and strips his shirt off. When he takes me in his arms again, our bodies are plastered together. My breasts smash against his hard chest. The ache in my nipples feels better when I rub against him. I writhe in his arms, sliding my body against his. Sean's hands trail down my back and cup my butt. He pulls me to him and lifts me out of the water. I wrap my legs around his waist and he carries me to the bed.

Looking into my eyes, he lays me back. "Tell me when to stop. I want you to like this, too."

I nod. My entire body is hypersensitive and craving his touch. As soon as his chest slips against me, I want his hands in places hands shouldn't go. My legs fall apart and Sean slips his fingers between them. He strokes me gently as he kisses me, finally slipping his finger inside of me. I push my hips into his hand, wanting more.

Sean pulls away, smiling and says, "Easy. Go slow. I don't want to hurt you."

I nod and lock eyes with him. I don't feel scared anymore. I just want him. I want to show him how he makes me feel when he looks at me with those sad eyes. I want to make him smile and I don't want it to stop. Taking his face between my hands, I pull him back down to my mouth. His hand slips between my thighs again and he presses inside me.

"Slowly," he says, pushing harder until I feel something pinch. I make a noise. It hurt a little, but I'm so turned on that I barely felt it. Sean stills his hand. "Are you all right?"

I nod and wiggle my hips against his hand. "Please," is the only coherent thought I have. My hips rock into his hand over and over again. A steady heat is building inside of me. If I don't have him inside me soon, I'll scream. Sean watches my body move as his hand turns me wanton. I manage to open my eyes and beg again, "Please."

It's like something inside him snaps. Sean moves and his hand is gone. I gasp, wanting it back. In a second, Sean is naked and on top of me. He strokes my hair away from my face and looks into my eyes. I feel his hard length pressing against my stomach. I want him between my legs. My mind is all lust. I tilt my hips against him, pressing into his leg.

"Are you sure you want this?" he asks.

I nod and suddenly feel like talking. I clutch at him, trying to pull him to me. "Please, Sean… please," I say, followed by a swarm of verbalized dirty wishes. I can't shut up. I know I'd never say anything like the stuff that's coming out of my mouth. I say dirtier things, things I didn't think I'd ever want before Sean placates me. His knee pushes my legs apart and he settles on top of me. One hand is on either side of my head, holding him up. I look at his spectacular body and have the impulse to lick it.

Sean says, "You're beautiful." I feel his dick between my legs. It rubs against me, making me crazy. I wrap my legs around his hips and push into him. He slides inside of me and I gasp. Sean stills as I get used to the feeling. "Are you okay?"

I nod. "Yes." Looking into his eyes, I put my hands on his ass and begin to rock. I do whatever my body tells me to, and right now it wants him deeper. I rock against him, wiggling my hips slowly, allowing the delicious sensations to overtake me completely. I have no idea who I am or what's happened to me. I forget all the pain that plagues my soul on a daily basis and lose myself in him.

Sean lowers his body on top of mine and begins to push in, then pulls out slowly, and pushes in again. The movement is so charged that I can't take it. I dig my nails into his back and rock violently against him. Sean pushes into me harder and faster. The feeling inside of my core grows hotter and wetter, finally exploding, sending surges through me. I cry out as I come, my nails clawing his back. Sean keeps rocking into me, drawing out the feeling. Every part of my body is sensitive. I feel everything. There's a throbbing inside of me. It grabs hold of his hard dick and fills me with happiness. A moment later, I feel him throbbing inside me. Innocently, I ask, "Did you come?"

He nods. "Did I hurt you? I wasn't going to, not this time, but oh my god—you're so sexy. I couldn't help myself."

I smile at him and push the dark hair away from his eyes. "I liked it."

"I'm glad." Sean pulls out of me slowly and I moan. I reach for him with a smile on my face. "Come back."

He smiles at me and kisses me on the forehead. "I'm not done with you, yet. I'm going to get you Advil and warm up that bath water. Are you up for a little sex in the water?"

"That sounds perfect." I lay naked on the bed when he goes to get me a pain killer. I take it and drink the bottle of water he hands me.

When Sean comes back, he walks toward me completely naked. This is the first time I've gotten to really look at him. His body is ripped, with perfectly sculpted muscles in his legs, arms, and chest. And his abs, oh my God, they're so tight, so perfect. The compulsion to lick them shoots through me again. My eyes drift lower, and I don't conceal my lust. I stare at his erection as he walks toward me, and press my thighs together hard to try and control myself.

"What's that look?" Sean asks, stopping before me. I'm lying on my back, on the bed with the sheets immodestly draped across my body. My hair is fanned around my face in long dark curls. His eyes slip over me and that warm feeling returns.

I smile lazily. It feels like I'm floating on a cloud. "I feel fluffy, like I could float away."

"You're happy, then?"

I nod, still smiling like nothing could pull me down from this high. Before I can say another word, Sean scoops me up in his arms. I don't expect it, so I yelp and giggle until I'm secure against his chest. His skin is so warm and smooth.

I press the spot along his shoulder, tracing my finger over his muscle as he walks me to the tub. "I want to run my tongue over this spot."

That makes him smile. Sean glances down at me in his arms. He steps into the marble bathroom and stops. He doesn't put my down. Looking into my eyes, he asks, "Is there anywhere else that little tongue of yours wants to go."

A mad blush turns my cheeks red. I don't know where it came from or why it happened. I bury my face in his shoulder, trying to hide. He laughs, "Apparently, so."

He steps over the side of the massive tub with me in his arms. I cling to Sean, hoping that he's more surefooted then me. I would have slipped. Sean plants both feet in the bottom of the tub and lowers me into the water, before sitting down himself. The tub is large enough to be a small pool. If I lay down, I could float and still have room before bumping into the walls. Sean sits opposite me and presses the button for the jets. He takes my hand with the bracelet and lowers it into the water.

"When I first saw you running down the side of the road, chasing your car, I never dreamed I'd end up doing this with you." His eyes are hungry again, like he can't get enough of me. "What did you think of me?"

I look at the froth on top of the water and say, "I thought you were hot and that I didn't have time for things like this. If someone told me that I'd be in bed with you tonight, I would have laughed my head off."

The thing is, I don't feel like laughing. I'm a call girl. This isn't real. This isn't what I wanted. I did what I had to do and was lucky enough to get him for a client.

THE ARRANGEMENT

VOL. 2

H.M. Ward

www.SexyAwesomeBooks.com

Laree Bailey Press

Copyright © 2013 by H.M. Ward
All rights reserved.

Laree Bailey Press
ISBN 1482628961
First Edition: Feb 2013

MORE ROMANCE BOOKS BY H.M. WARD

SCANDALOUS

SCANDALOUS 2

DAMAGED

SECRETS

VALENTINE'S KISSES

THE SECRET LIFE OF TRYSTAN SCOTT

And more.

To see a full book list, please visit:

www.SexyAwesomeBooks.com/books.htm

CAN'T WAIT FOR H.M WARD'S
NEXT STEAMY BOOK?

Let her know by leaving stars and telling her what you liked about THE ARRANGEMENT VOL. 2 in a review!